THE
SHERLOCK HOLMES
CHILDREN'S COLLECTION
MYSTERY, MISCHIEF AND MAYHEM

Published by Sweet Cherry Publishing Limited
Unit 36, Vulcan House,
Vulcan Road,
Leicester, LE5 3EF
United Kingdom

First published in the UK in 2020
2020 edition

2 4 6 8 10 9 7 5 3 1

ISBN: 978-1-78226-424-8

Sherlock Holmes: Charles Augustus Milverton

Based on the original story from Sir Arthur Conan Doyle,
adapted by Stephanie Baudet.

Cover design by Arianna Bellucci and Rhiannon Izard
Illustrations by Arianna Bellucci

www.sweetcherrypublishing.com

Printed and bound in China
C.WM004

SHERLOCK HOLMES

CHARLES AUGUSTUS MILVERTON

SIR ARTHUR CONAN DOYLE

I am going to tell you a story that happened many years ago ...

It was a cold, frosty, winter's evening. Holmes and I had been out for one of our evening walks. We got back to Baker Street at about six o'clock.

We went into our sitting room and took off our outdoor clothes. Holmes turned up the lamp. By its light we saw a small card on the table. He gave a shout of disgust and then swept it onto the floor.

I was surprised at his reaction and picked it up.

It read:

CHARLES AUGUSTUS MILVERTON
ART AGENT
Appledore Towers,
Hampstead

'Who is he?' I asked.

'The worst man in London,' Holmes answered. He sat down

and stretched his legs out in front
of the fire. 'Is there anything on
the back of the card?'

I turned it over.

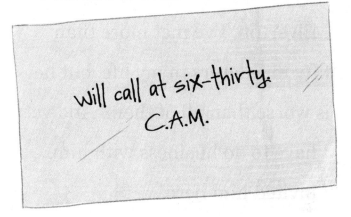

will call at six-thirty.
C.A.M.

'Hmm. He'll be here soon.
Tell me, Watson, do you have a
creeping, shrinking feeling when
you watch the snakes in the zoo?

When you see the slithery
creatures, with their deadly eyes
and wicked, flattened faces?
Well, that's how I feel when I see
Milverton. I've met more than
fifty murderers in my life, but he
is worse than all of them. And yet
I have to do business with him.
I invited him here.'

I was curious but also a little
sickened by Holmes' description.

'But who is he?' I asked.

'I'll tell you, Watson. He is the

king of all the blackmailers. He has a smiling face, but his heart is made of cold, hard marble. He will squeeze and squeeze a person, until he has taken every last drop of their money.'

My heart sank. I did not want to meet such a horrible person.

Holmes continued. 'The man is a genius, really. He could

Blackmailer

A blackmailer is a person who steals secrets and then demands to be paid large amounts of money, gifts or favours, not to reveal them. Blackmailers are usually very cunning, and so can be extremely tricky to catch.

have been a great person if he had chosen a more honest job. This is what he does: he lets everyone know that he will pay a lot of money for personal letters. Any letters that will harm the good name of rich and important people. He gets these letters from household staff or con men.'

I listened to Holmes with horror.

'Milverton is not mean with his payments. He once paid seven hundred pounds to a footman for a very short note. But that note was enough to ruin a whole noble family. Once he has the letters in his slimy hands, he demands to be paid a huge amount of money. If the rich and important people do not pay, he promises to release the letters to the public and ruin their reputation forever.

'There are hundreds of people in this great city who turn pale when they hear his name. No one knows where he will strike next. He is far too rich and too cunning to be reckless. He will keep a letter for years so that he can use it when it is worth the most.

'I have said that he is the worst man in London. He is not a brute, who hits his friends when he's angry. A brute would be easy to take down. This man calmly destroys people just to get richer and richer. He cannot be harmed and is almost impossible to stop.'

I had not heard my friend speak like this before. But I had not heard of this evil man, either.

'But surely the man is breaking the law?' I asked.

'Yes, he is. But what is the point of putting him in prison for a few months? Milverton would find and ruin the person who put him there. His victims do not dare to strike back – they are too afraid of him. If ever he blackmailed an innocent person, someone who had no secrets to hide, then we would have him. But he is as cunning as the devil. No, we must find other ways to fight him.'

'And why is he coming here?'

'Because a well-known client has asked for my help,' said Holmes. 'It is Lady Eva Brackwell. She will marry the Earl of Dovercourt in two weeks. Milverton has stolen letters of hers, that she sent to a previous boyfriend. He was a poor young man. She loved him, but he could not earn enough money to feed them both. It would have been an impossible marriage, anyway. Her family would not

have allowed it. Milverton said
he will send the love letters to
the earl unless she pays him a lot
of money. I have been asked to
meet him, to sort it out.'

I had not heard of this lady, but
I felt sorry for her. She had to give
up the man she loved because he
was poor and seen as unimportant.
Now she risked losing the rich
earl too, if he saw the love letters.

Suddenly, there was a clatter
and a rattle in the street below.

I looked down from the window and saw a beautiful carriage. It had bright, shining sidelamps, which gleamed on the glossy backs of the two chestnut horses pulling it.

A footman opened the door and a small, tubby man climbed out. He was wearing a thick overcoat. We heard the doorbell ring, and then Mrs Hudson, our housekeeper, showed him in.

A minute later he was at the door. Holmes opened it.

17

Charles Augustus Milverton was fifty years old. He had a large head, a round, plump, hairless face and a frozen smile. His grey eyes shone brightly from behind his round, gold-edged glasses.

He stepped forwards and reached out a plump little hand. He said he was sorry he had missed us on his first visit and hoped we had seen the card he left on the table. His voice was smooth, but not kind.

Holmes ignored the hand
and looked at him with a face
of stone. Milverton's smile
widened. He wasn't at all hurt by
Holmes not shaking his hand. He
shrugged, took off his coat and

folded it carefully over the back
of a chair. Then he sat down,
without being asked.

'This man,' Milverton said, with
a wave in my direction. 'Can he
be trusted not to talk?'

'Doctor Watson is my friend
and partner,' said Holmes.

'Very good, Mr Holmes.
I would not want your client's
secret to be spread about. It is so
very private,' Milverton said,
still smiling.

The nerve of the man! I felt so shocked and angry, I could have flung him out there and then. But Holmes was more professional. He seemed calm, though his face was as hard as steel.

'Doctor Watson already knows about it.'

'Then we can get down to business.' Milverton carefully took off his gloves and laid them neatly on the arm of the chair. His movements were smooth and snake-like. Just like Holmes had said. 'You say that you are acting for Lady Eva? Has she asked you to accept my deal?'

'What is your deal?'

'I want seven thousand pounds.'

'Otherwise, what will happen?'

'My dear sir, it is painful for me to talk about it. If the money is not paid by the fourteenth of this month, there will be no marriage on the eighteenth.' His smile was more smug than ever.

Holmes looked thoughtful for a moment. 'You are taking too much for granted,' he said. 'I know what is in these letters and my client will do what I advise. I will tell her to tell her future husband the whole story. I'm sure he will understand and forgive her.'

Milverton chuckled. 'You do not know the earl.'

Holmes looked baffled. 'What harm is there in the letters?' he asked.

'They are very personal,' Milverton answered. 'The lady is a good letter writer. I can tell you that the Earl of Dovercourt would be shocked. But do as you like. If you think that it is a good idea for Lady Eva to give the letters to the earl, then fine. It would be silly for her to pay so much money to get them back.'

He stood up and reached for his coat.

Holmes was grey with anger. His face was shaking as if about to explode.

'Wait a moment,' he said, trying to keep his voice calm. 'You go too fast. We still want to avoid a scandal.'

Milverton sat back down in the chair. 'I was sure that you would see it that way,' he purred.

Holmes continued, 'Lady Eva is not a rich lady. Even two thousand pounds would be difficult for her to get. The amount you want is impossible. Please agree to give back the letters for less money.'

Milverton's smile widened and his eyes twinkled.

'I know it is true that she is not a rich lady. But surely when a lady is getting married it is normal for her friends and family to give a little money as a wedding present. I am sure she would get more than enough to pay my debt. And this little bundle of letters would give her more joy than all the water glasses and butter-dishes in London.'

'It is impossible,' said Holmes.

'Dear me, that's too bad!' cried Milverton, taking a wallet out of his pocket. 'I can't help thinking that people are foolish not to try to pay. Look at this!' He held up a little note with a coat-of-arms on the envelope. 'That belongs to … well, perhaps it's not fair to tell you her name until tomorrow

morning. At that time, this letter will be in the hands of her husband. And all because she will not pay me. It's such a small amount of money, she could get it just by selling her diamonds. But, no. It is *such* a pity.'

He put the letter back into his wallet and looked at us both. 'Now, do you remember when the Honourable Miss Miles and Colonel Dorking suddenly ended their engagement? It was only two days before the wedding. It was reported in the *Morning Post*. And why? Because they did not pay me. A tiny sum of one thousand pounds would have stopped all those nasty secrets from getting out. Is it not terrible? And here I find you, a sensible man, arguing about money when your client's future is at stake. You surprise me, Mr Holmes.'

I could hardly contain my hatred of the man. I remembered

reading about that sad news in

the *Morning Post.*

The marriage of the Honourable Miss Charlotte Miles to Colonel Edward Dorking, has been cancelled for unknown reasons.

Gifts will be returned.

Servicem… have bee… Every ef… redunda… local for… Order ha… calamity… keep all

'What I say is true,' Holmes

replied. 'The money cannot be

found. Surely it is better for you

31

to just take the money that I offer.
Ruining this woman's future
cannot help you in any way. No
one will pay you for doing that.'

'Incorrect, Mr Holmes,'
Milverton said. 'Telling her secret
would help me. I have around ten
people's secret letters just waiting
for the right moment. If I ruin
Lady Eva's marriage, those people
will know I'm serious. Then they
will be far more likely to pay up.
Do you see?'

Holmes sprang from his chair.

'Get behind him, Watson!' he shouted. 'Don't let him out! Now, sir, let us see what is in that wallet.'

Milverton had glided like a snake to the side of the room. He stood with his back against the wall.

'Mr Holmes, Mr Holmes,' he said, calmly. He pulled back the front of his waistcoat and showed us a large gun that was sticking out from his pocket. 'I was expecting you to do something original. I have been trapped so many times. And what good has ever come from it? I am armed to the teeth and am not scared to use my weapons. Besides, I would not be foolish enough to bring the letters with me. But now, gentlemen, I have one or two other

appointments this evening. And it is a long drive to Hampstead, so I must be off.'

He stepped forward and picked up his coat. Then he laid his hand on his gun, and turned to the door.

I had picked up a chair but Holmes shook his head. I laid it down again.

With a bow and a smile, Milverton left the room. A few moments later we heard the slam of the carriage door. Then there was a rattle of the wheels as he drove away.

Holmes sat by the fire without moving. His hands were buried deep in his trouser pockets. His chin sat on his chest and his eyes stared at the glowing embers of the fire.

For half an hour he sat silent and still. Then, all of a sudden, he seemed to make a decision. He sprang to his feet and went into his bedroom. A little later, a young workman with a small beard and a swagger walked out. It was Holmes in a perfect disguise!

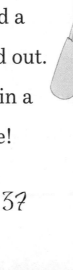

He lit his clay pipe on the lamp.

'I'll be back soon, Watson,' he said. Then he walked down the stairs, opened the front door and vanished into the night.

I knew then that he had begun his fight against Charles Augustus Milverton. But I never dreamed how it would turn out.

For thirteen days, Holmes used this disguise. I didn't know what he was doing. He only told me that he was in Hampstead.

At last, on a wild, stormy evening, he returned from his last outing. He took off his disguise and sat in front of the fire. He chuckled quietly to himself.

'Would you call me a marrying man, Watson?'

'No, certainly not!'

'Then you'll be interested to hear that I am engaged.'

'My dear fellow! I ...'

'To Milverton's housemaid.'

'Good heavens, Holmes!'

The idea that Holmes was engaged
seemed unlikely, but, for a moment,
I had been glad.

'I wanted information, Watson.'

'Surely you have gone too far?' I said. I thought of the poor girl he was using to get his information.

'I had to do it, Watson. I am pretending to be a plumber called Mr Escott. I have seen the girl each evening and we have taken a walk together and talked. I have got all the information I wanted. I now know Milverton's house like the palm of my hand.'

'But the girl, Holmes. You have got her love and will now drop her.'

I'm sure that the tone of my voice showed that I did not like the idea.

He shrugged.

'You are right that it is not fair, Watson. But I must use any way I can to get information. There is so much at stake. Plus, I have a rival for her love. Another man has been speaking to her, so I'm sure she will soon turn her love to him instead. Ah, what a wonderful night it is.'

I glanced at the rain-spattered windows. 'You like this weather?'

'It suits my purpose. Watson, I am going to burgle Milverton's house tonight.'

I caught my breath. My skin went cold at the words. Suddenly, like a flash of lightning at night, I had a vision. I saw in my mind what could happen after this burglary. Holmes could be caught and his great career would end in failure and disgrace. He would be at the mercy of the horrible Milverton.

'For heaven's sake, Holmes, think about what you are doing!' I cried.

'My dear fellow, I have thought about it for a long time. I never act hastily. I wouldn't do anything so dangerous if there were another way.'

He looked at me.

'Let us look at the matter clearly and fairly. Would you agree that beating Milverton is the right thing to do? Even though it's a crime? Burgling his house is no worse than taking his wallet by force. And you were going to help me do that.'

I thought about it for a moment. It was a crime to break into a house. But if it saved a young lady from losing her husband, then that was a good reason.

'Yes, I suppose,' I said. 'So long as we only take the letters he would use to destroy people.'

'Exactly. It is a crime, but it will help Lady Eva. I just have to think about the personal risk. But surely a gentleman should not think too much of personal risk when a lady needs help?'

'You will be in such a horrible position, Holmes.'

'Well, that is part of the risk. But, there is no other possible

way of getting these letters back.
The poor lady has not got enough
money to pay Milverton. And
she has no one else to help her.
Tomorrow is the last day. Unless
we can get the letters tonight,
the villain will send them to her
fiancé. He will ruin her life.'

I nodded.

'I can either let her be ruined
or make this last effort to help,'
Holmes went on. 'Watson, it's like
a duel between Milverton and me.

47

He won the first round. But my self-respect and good name force me to fight it to the finish.'

'Well, I don't like it, but I suppose it must happen,' I said. 'When do we start?'

'You are not coming.'

'Then you are not going,' I said. 'I give you my word that I will take a cab straight to the police station. I will tell them that you are going to rob the house, unless you let me share this adventure with you.'

Holmes looked at me, smiling.

'Not against a little blackmail yourself, Watson?' He chuckled. 'But you can't help me.'

'How do you know that? You don't know what will happen. Anyway, my mind is made up.

Other people besides you have
self-respect and good names
to uphold.'

Holmes frowned at first, but
then his face softened. He clapped
me on the shoulder.

'Well, well, my dear fellow, so
be it. We have shared the same
rooms for some years. It would be
very funny if we ended up sharing
the same prison cell. You know,
Watson, I don't mind telling you
that I have always thought that I

would make a great criminal. This is my chance to find out. See here!'

He took a neat little leather case out of a drawer and opened it. He showed me a group of shining tools. 'This is a first class, up-to-date burgling kit. It has a jemmy, a diamond-tipped glass cutter, adaptable keys, and every other gadget that we need.

Jemmy
A short, curved metal bar that is used to force open locked windows or doors. Most burglars will carry a jemmy and use it to break into the homes of rich people, and steal whatever treasures they find there.

And here is my dark lantern. Everything is in order. Do you have a pair of silent shoes?'

'I have rubber-soled tennis shoes.'

'Excellent. And a mask?'

'I can make a couple out of black silk.'

'You have a natural talent for this sort of thing, Watson.' He gave me one of his half smiles. 'You make the masks. We shall have some cold supper before we start. It's now nine-thirty. At eleven o'clock we shall drive as far as Church Row. It is a fifteen minute walk from there to Appledore Towers. We shall be at work before midnight. Milverton is a heavy sleeper. He goes to bed at exactly ten-thirty. With any luck we should be back here by two o'clock with Lady Eva's letters in my pocket.'

Holmes and I put on our evening dress clothes, so that we looked as if we were on our way home from the theatre. In Oxford Street we picked up a cab and drove to an address in Hampstead. Then we paid off our cab and walked along the edge of the Heath. We had buttoned up our coats as it was bitterly cold.

The wind seemed to blow right through us.

'This could be tricky,' said Holmes. 'The papers are kept in a safe in Milverton's study and the study is next to his bedroom. On the other hand, he is a very deep sleeper.

Agatha – that's my fiancée – says it's a joke among the servants that it's impossible to wake the master. He has a secretary who never leaves the study all day. That's why we are going at night. He also has a beast of a dog that roams the garden. I met Agatha late here the last two evenings. She locks the dog up now to make sure he doesn't chase me.'

I had a strange image of Holmes pretending to charm a

young lady, while actually trying to take note of everything in the house and garden.

We stopped. 'This is the house: this big one, in its own land,' said Holmes. We went through the gate. 'Now, turn to the right, and duck behind the laurel bushes. We can put on our masks here, I think. There's not a glimmer of light in any of the windows, Watson. Everything is working well.'

We pulled our black silk masks on and turned into two of the most suspicious-looking people in London. We crept up to the silent, gloomy house. A tiled path extended along one side of it, lined by several windows and two doors.

58

'That's his bedroom,' Holmes whispered, pointing at a window. 'This door opens straight into his study.' He tried the handle. 'But it is bolted and locked – we would make too much noise getting in. Come round here. There's a conservatory that opens into the drawing room. We can sneak through the house, to the study.'

The conservatory door was locked, too. Holmes got out his diamond glass cutter from his burgling kit and cut a neat circle of glass out of the door. Then he reached in and unlocked it from the inside. As soon as we were in, Holmes closed the door behind us. We had become criminals in the eyes of the law.

The thick, warm air of the conservatory and the rich, choking smell of exotic plants made us gasp. Holmes grabbed my hand in the darkness. He led me swiftly past groups of small

plants that brushed
against our faces.
Over the years,
Holmes had developed
an amazing power to
see in the dark.

Still holding my hand, he opened a door. I could just about see that we had entered a large room. The smell of cigar smoke told me that someone had been smoking here not long before. Holmes felt his way among the furniture, to another door. He opened it, stepped through, and then closed it behind us.

I reached out my hand and felt lots of coats hanging from the wall. We were in a passage. We walked silently along it. Holmes very gently opened a door on the right-hand side. Something rushed out at us. My heart sprang into my mouth! I could have laughed out loud when I saw that it was a cat.

A fire was burning in this room. The air was heavy with cigar smoke. Holmes walked in on tiptoe. He waited for me to follow, and then very gently closed the door. We were in Milverton's study. A small door on the far side showed the way to his bedroom.

It was a good fire. The room was lit up by it. Near the door I saw the gleam of an electric switch, but it was not safe to turn it on

– the light would give us away.
At one side of the fireplace was
a heavy curtain, covering a bay
window. On the other side was
the door that led out to the tiled
path, which we had tried to get

through moments before. A desk
stood in the centre of the room.
It had a huge, red leather swivel

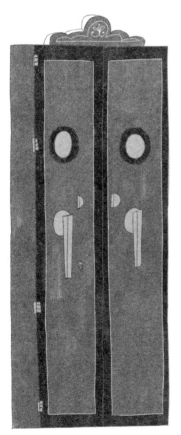 chair sat behind it.
Opposite, was a large
bookcase, and in
the corner, between
the bookcase and
the wall, stood a
tall green safe. The
polished brass knobs
on its front shone in
the firelight.

Holmes crept across and looked at it. Then he went to the door of the bedroom and pressed his ear to it, listening intently. No sound came from inside. Meanwhile, I thought I would plan our escape route. I tiptoed over to unlock the door that opened onto the veranda. But, to my amazement, it was not locked or bolted! It definitely had been a minute ago. I touched Holmes on the arm and he turned his masked face to the door. I saw him jump slightly – he was surprised as I was.

'I don't like it,' he whispered, his mouth close to my ear. 'I don't know how it was opened, or who by. But we can't stand here and think – we have no time to lose.'

'Can I do anything?'

'Yes. Stand by the door. If you hear anyone coming from the outside, lock the door. We can escape the same way we came. If they come through the house, we

can get through the outside door.
But only if we have the letter.
If we haven't, we'll have to hide
behind these curtains until they
leave. Then we will continue our
mission. Do you understand?'

I nodded and stood by the door.
I was scared before, but now I
just felt excited. We would be in
a lot of trouble if we were caught.
Our mission, however, was too
important to fail. Knowing that
it was a brave and unselfish act

made the adventure even more thrilling.

Far from feeling guilty, I enjoyed the danger. I watched Holmes in amazement. He was so calm. He unrolled his burglary kit and chose his tool, as if he was a surgeon about to perform a tricky operation. I knew that he enjoyed opening safes – it was a hobby of his. To be faced by this green and gold monster was almost a treat. He would defeat this metal dragon that held in its jaws the good name of many fair ladies.

Holmes had placed his coat over a chair and now turned up the cuffs of his jacket. He laid out two drills, a jemmy, and several keys.

I stood at the centre door, keeping watch. I told myself I was ready for any emergency. Although, I didn't quite know what I would do if there was one.

For half an hour Holmes worked on the safe. He would

71

lay down one tool, pick up another, and handle each with the strength of a trained mechanic.

Finally, I heard a click. The wide green door swung open. Inside, I could see a number of paper packets. Each was tied, sealed and labelled. Holmes picked one out, but it was hard to read by the flickering fire. He took out his little lantern. Suddenly I saw him stop and listen. In an instant, he had swung the door of the safe closed. He picked up his coat, stuffed his tools into his pockets, and darted behind the curtains. He jerked his head, to tell me to do the same.

There was a noise somewhere in the house – a quiet murmur. A door slammed in the distance. Then the quiet murmur grew louder and louder. It was the thud of footsteps. They were coming this way. They were in the passage outside the room.

The footsteps
stopped. The study
door opened. There
was a sharp click as
the electric light was
turned on. The door
closed again, and the
strong smell of cigar
smoke drifted up
my nose. Then the
footsteps continued,
backwards and
forwards, backwards

75

and forwards. My heart was in my mouth. I was holding my breath, afraid of letting it out in case I made a noise.

Finally, there was a creak from a chair, and the footsteps stopped. Then a key clicked in a lock and I heard the rustle of papers.

Very gently, I breathed out. I wanted to see what was going on. So I carefully parted the curtains and peeped through. I could feel Holmes' shoulder against mine,

and I knew that he
was watching too.

Right in front of
us was the broad,
rounded back of
Milverton. He was

so close that we could almost touch him. It was clear that we had made a mistake about his movements. He had never been in his bedroom. He had been sitting in another room, on the other side of the house. That was why we had not seen any lighted windows.

I fixed my eyes on Milverton's large, bald head, which shone in the firelight. He was leaning back in the red leather chair, his legs outstretched. He had a long, black cigar sticking out of his mouth.

He wore a dark red smoking jacket with a black velvet collar. In his hand he had a long, important-looking paper. He read it slowly, blowing out rings of smoke from time to time. I could see that he was not in a hurry to move.

I felt Holmes take my hand again and give it a shake. It was as if to say that everything was all right and there was no need to worry.

But I was not sure whether he had seen what I had seen.

The door of the safe was not properly closed.

At any moment, Milverton could look up and see it. I decided that, if he noticed it, I would spring out. I'd throw my coat over him, and pin him to the ground. Then I would leave the rest to Holmes.

But Milverton never looked up. He lazily turned the pages of the papers in his hand.

At least, I thought,
when he has finished the
document and the cigar he
will go to his bedroom.

But before he had finished
either, something happened.

He had been looking at his
watch a lot. Once, he even stood
up, paced, and then sat back
down again. He was waiting
for something. But surely he
wouldn't have somewhere to go at
this late hour?

81

From somewhere in the house a clock chimed twelve. The last tones had just died away when I heard a faint sound from the path, outside. Milverton dropped his papers and sat straight in his chair. I heard the sound again. Then there came a gentle tap at the door.

Milverton got up and opened it.

'Well,' he said sharply, 'you are nearly half an hour late.'

So, this was why the door was

unlocked. And why Milverton was still awake.

There was the gentle rustle of a woman's dress. I had closed the slit between the curtains, in case Milverton saw us. But now I very carefully opened it again. He had sat down again and the cigar was still sticking out of the corner of his mouth. In front of him, in the full glare of the electric light, stood a tall, slim, dark woman. She had a veil over her face and

a cloak pulled around her chin. She was breathing quickly, and every inch of her body was shaking.

'You've made me lose a good night's rest, my dear,' said Milverton. 'I hope it will be worth it.

You couldn't come at any other time, eh?'

The woman shook her head.

'Well, if you couldn't, you couldn't. You said the countess is a horrible boss. This is your chance to get even with her. Bless you, girl, why are you shivering? Pull yourself together! Now, let's get down to business.'

He took a note from the drawer of his desk. I peered at it and could just read the large writing.

Sir,

I have five letters that belong to the Countess d'Albert. They are personal and private. She would not want them made public. I want to sell them. I shall come to your house at eleven-thirty tonight.

Her Ladyship's personal maid.

Milverton waved the letter at her. 'So far, so good,' he said. 'All that's left is for me to fix a price. I would want to see the letters, of course. If they are really good specimens … Good heavens, is it you?'

Without a word, the woman had taken off her veil. She had a dark, handsome face, with a curved nose, strong, dark eyebrows, glittering eyes, and a straight, thin-lipped mouth. A mouth that was set in a dangerous smile.

'It is I,' she said, 'the woman whose life you have ruined.'

Milverton laughed but I could hear a hint of fear in his voice. 'You were very stubborn. Why

did you make me do such a thing? Honestly, I wouldn't normally hurt a fly. But every man has his business, and what could I do? I only asked for a little money. I knew you could pay, but you did not.'

'I did not,' the

woman said, staring so firmly at Milverton that she barely blinked. 'So two weeks ago, you sent the letters to my husband. He was the finest man that ever lived. It broke his heart, and he died. He was a man whose boots I was never even good enough to lace …' Her voice shook with sadness but she went on.

'Do you remember that last night? When I came through that door and I begged you for mercy?

You laughed in my face as you are trying to laugh now. Only, now, your cowardly heart cannot keep your lips from twitching. You are scared. You never thought you would see me here again, did you? But it was that night that showed me that I was brave enough to meet you face to face, and alone. Well, Charles Milverton, what do you have to say?'

'You cannot bully me,' he said, rising to his feet. 'I only have to call my servants and they will have you arrested in minutes. But I will forgive your anger. It's only natural. Leave now, and I will say no more.'

The woman stood with her head bowed and the same deadly smile on her thin lips.

'You will ruin no more lives as you ruined mine. You will break no more hearts as you broke mine. I will free the world of your poison.'

From under her cloak she drew out a small gun and pointed it at Milverton.

'Take that, you hound! And that, and that!'

She fired shot after shot into his body.

Milverton fell forwards onto the table, coughing and clawing at the papers. He tried to stagger to his feet, but was shot

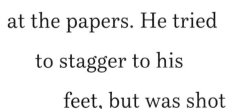

again, and collapsed onto
the floor.

The woman stared at his still
body.

There was nothing we could
have done to save him. When the
woman was shooting Milverton,
I wanted to spring out, but I felt
Holmes' cold, strong grasp on
my wrist. I understood what that
grip meant. It meant that we
should not interrupt. This was
not our problem. Justice had

caught up with the villain. We should not forget the mission we came to complete.

The woman took one last look at Milverton's body before stepping out into the night. Not even a second passed before we heard voices echoing across the house. Feet were hurrying towards the study. The gunshots had awoken Milverton's servants.

Holmes leapt out from behind the curtain. With swift, silent steps,

he walked over to the other door.
He turned the key in the lock.

Then, with perfect coolness,
Holmes ran across
to the safe. He filled
both his arms with
bundles of letters
and threw them
into the fire. Again
and again he did
it, until the safe
was empty.

Someone turned the handle and banged on the door, trying to get in. Holmes quickly scanned the room with his eyes. The letter that had caused the death of Milverton was still on the table, all spattered with his blood. Holmes tossed it into the blazing fire too. Then he took the key from the outer door, and followed me through it, out onto the tiled path. He locked the door behind us.

'This way, Watson. We can climb the garden wall and escape,' he said, dashing into the bushes.

The news spread quickly. Looking back as we ran, every window in the house was lit. The front door was open and people were rushing down the drive. The whole garden was alive with maids, cooks, butlers and footmen. One man gave a great shout as he spotted us and began to run towards us.

Holmes seemed to know the grounds perfectly. He ran swiftly through the small trees. I was close at his heels. The man was still chasing us, but he was panting hard and falling behind.

The garden wall was six-foot high, but Holmes easily pulled himself up and over it. I did the same. I had one foot on top of the wall and was just about to pull the other up when I felt the man

grab my ankle. I tried to shake
him off, but I was losing my grip.
I didn't want to think about what
would happen if he managed
to pull me down.

The fear gave me extra strength. I kicked out with my trapped foot. The man yelped as my heel struck his face and he let go of my ankle. I scrambled over the moss-covered wall and fell into the bushes on the other side.

Holmes pulled me to my feet and together we dashed away across Hampstead Heath. I had no idea if the man was still following us. It is amazing how the body finds extra energy when it's needed. I had never run so fast or for so long as I did that night.

We had run two miles, I suppose, when Holmes at last stopped. We stood gasping, slowly getting our breath back. There was absolute silence behind us. We had shaken off our followers and were safe.

I grinned in the darkness. 'You are very fit, Holmes. It's surprising since you get so little exercise.'

'As are you, Watson. It must be all that tennis that you play.'

We made our way home and were glad to sink into our beds. The following morning, we had just finished breakfast when there was a knock at the door. Mr Lestrade, of Scotland Yard, was shown into our sitting room. He looked very serious.

'Good morning, Mr Holmes, Doctor Watson,' he said. 'Are you busy right now?'

'Not too busy to listen to you,' replied Holmes.

'I thought that if you had nothing special to do, you could help me on a case. It is a very strange case. It happened only last night in Hampstead.'

'Dear me,' said Holmes. 'What was that?'

'A murder, a most dramatic and amazing murder. I know how keen you are on these things. It would be a great favour if you would go to Appledore Towers and give us your advice. It is no ordinary crime. We have had our eyes on this Mr Milverton for some time. He was a bit of a villain. Apparently, he held papers that he used for blackmailing purposes. These papers have all been burnt by the murderers. No money or valuables were taken. We think the men's only aim was to prevent the secrets from getting out.'

'Murderers!' cried Holmes. 'Plural!'

'Yes, there were two of them. They were almost caught red-handed. We have their footprints and their description. I'm sure we will catch them. The first fellow was very active. But the second man was caught by the gardener as he climbed the wall. He only got away after a struggle. He was a middle-sized, strongly-built man. He had a square jaw, thick neck, moustache, and a mask over his eyes.'

'That's not very clear,' said Holmes, and turned to me with a glint in his eye. 'Why, it could be a description of Watson!'

'It's true,' said the inspector, smiling. 'It could well be a description of Watson.'

'Well, I'm afraid I can't help you, Lestrade,' said Holmes. 'The fact is that I knew this fellow, Milverton. He was one of the most dangerous men in London. I think there are certain crimes that the law cannot touch. Private revenge is acceptable in these cases. No, don't argue. I have made up my mind. I think the criminals must have had a good reason to kill him. I will not handle this case.'

Holmes and I had not talked about what happened the night before. But all morning I saw that he was in his a very thoughtful mood. His eyes were empty, as if he were trying to remember something.

We were in the middle of our lunch when he suddenly sprang to his feet.

'By Jove, Watson! I know who she was!' Holmes cried. 'Get your hat! Come with me!'

We hurried at top speed down Baker Street, then along Oxford Street until we had almost reached Regent Circus. On the left was a shop window filled with photographs of celebrities. Holmes fixed his eyes on one of them.

It was a regal-looking lady in a very smart dress. She had a tall diamond tiara on her noble head.

I looked at her delicately-curved nose, her neat eyebrows, her straight mouth and the strong little chin beneath it. Beneath the picture was her name and the name of the great nobleman whose wife she had been. I gasped.

I looked at Holmes. He put his finger to his lips as we turned away from the window and walked on.

Sherlock Holmes

World-renowned private detective Sherlock Holmes has solved hundreds of mysteries, and is the author of such fascinating monographs as *Early English Charters* and *The Influence of a Trade Upon the Form of a Hand.* He keeps bees in his free time.

Dr John Watson

Wounded in action at Maiwand, Dr John Watson left the army and moved into 221B Baker Street. There he was surprised to learn that his new friend, Sherlock Holmes, faced daily peril solving crimes, and began documenting his investigations.
Dr Watson also runs a doctor's practice.